Katie IN LONDON

JAMES MAYHEW

ORCHARD

For Max
~ a story about your Mum ~

ORCHARD BOOKS
Carmelite House
50 Victoria Embankment
London EC4Y 0DZ

ISBN 978 1 40833 193 4

First published in 2003 by Orchard Books
First published in paperback in 2004
This edition published in 2014

8 10 9

Printed in China

Orchard Books
An imprint of Hachette Children's Group
Part of The Watts Publishing Group Limited
An Hachette UK Company
www.hachette.co.uk

FSC
www.fsc.org
MIX
Paper from
responsible sources
FSC® C104740

LONDON SEEMED VERY BIG to Katie. Big trains, big buildings and big crowds. She held on to Grandma with one hand and her little brother, Jack, with the other. They all got onto a big red bus and set off to see the sights.

When they got off at Trafalgar Square,
Grandma was tired.
"I'll just have a little rest," she yawned. "You two
stay by that lion, then I'll know where you are."

Katie climbed onto the big bronze lion and pulled Jack up after her. As the sun came out, the lion seemed to turn from grey to gold. "Do you mind?" said a very deep voice. It was the lion! "Who said you could clamber all over me?"

"We're very sorry," said Katie. "Grandma said to stay with you." "Then I suppose you must," sighed the lion. "Now, what shall we do?" "We wanted to see the sights, but Grandma fell asleep," said Katie. "Could you take us?" "Oh yes, please do!" said Jack.

The lion shook his mane.
"Hold on tight!" he roared,
bounding out of Trafalgar Square.

How people stared! But the lion didn't mind.
"This is much better than lying on that stone all day,"
he said. "You have no idea how cold my tummy gets.
Now, where shall we go?"
"You choose!" laughed Katie and Jack.

The lion took them to St Paul's Cathedral.
They gazed up at the enormous dome.
"It makes me feel very small," said Jack.
"It's so tall it makes me feel dizzy,"
laughed the lion. "Come on, let's go.
There is so much I want
to show you!"

Next, the lion took Katie and Jack to an old castle.

"The Tower of London," he said. "Haunted by
the ghosts of kings and queens."

Katie shivered.

"Don't worry, they only come out after midnight,"
said the lion. "But you can see their crowns and jewels."

The Crown Jewels were in a small, special room.
It was quite a tight squeeze for the lion. The
jewels sparkled like stars in a night sky, but
in all sorts of colours – green emeralds,
red rubies and blue sapphires.

Afterwards, the lion pretended he was
a ghost and chased Katie and Jack.
"Excuse me," called a man in an old-fashioned
costume. "You're scaring my ravens!"
"Who's he?" whispered Katie.
"He's a Yeoman Warder," said the lion.
"He believes that the towers will fall down
if the ravens leave. Time to go!"

The lion decided to take them
across the River Thames. They
trotted onto Tower Bridge.
Suddenly an alarm sounded
and lights flashed.

A boat was coming and the bridge was being raised to let it through. "Stop!" yelled Katie. But the lion didn't stop – he jumped!

But instead of landing on the other side, they landed on
the boat. They chugged along the river, passing great
ships and going under dark bridges.

"Look! That's the Globe Theatre," said the lion. "Shakespeare wrote some fine plays that are performed there to this day, although very few of them have lions in them."

"What's that big wheel over there?" asked Jack.
"It must be the London Eye," said Katie. "Why don't we go on it?"
"You don't expect me to go on that thing do you?" said the lion, as they all jumped off the boat onto the South Bank.

Before the lion could say another word, Katie bustled him
on board the London Eye.
Slowly the wheel turned and they rose high above London.
The poor lion turned rather pale and began to shake, but soon
even he couldn't help enjoying the view. He pointed to Big Ben.
"Goodness, it's nearly eleven o'clock. We must hurry!"

As they came down, Big Ben chimed eleven times. Katie and Jack jumped onto the lion and they raced across a bridge, past the huge clock and the Houses of Parliament.

They hopped in and out of queues of traffic, past taxis
and red double-decker buses, past parks and grand
buildings. They could hear music and drums.

"It's the Changing of the Guard!" said the lion. "Follow me – left, right, left, right . . . " The lion marched off behind the guardsmen, in time to the music. Katie and Jack followed, all the way to the gates of Buckingham Palace.

"Sorry," said a policeman, "only Royal
Guards are allowed through here."
So Katie and Jack jumped back up,
and the lion walked on, past
the palace.

They hoped to see a real prince or princess. Instead, they noticed a lot of flags and crests with lions on them. The lion smiled. "I'm very well known by the Royal Family." "Why is that?" asked Katie. "Because the lion is called the King of the Beasts!" he said, proudly.

And as they galloped away, perhaps they did catch a glimpse of someone waving from a palace window?

By now the lion's paws were beginning to ache, so they all went to sit in a leafy park. The lion dangled his paws in a cool lake. Jack bought ice creams with his pocket money.

"Delicious!" said the lion. "I love tutti-frutti!"

"How are your paws?" asked Katie.

"Rather sore," admitted the lion. "I'm not used to all this walking. Perhaps we could catch a bus back to Trafalgar Square?"

A policeman told them to catch
a number nine bus from Harrods,
the big department store.
"I wish I didn't have to go back,"
said the lion, sadly.
"Don't you like Trafalgar
Square?" asked Katie.

"Of course," said the lion,
"but I do get such a very cold
tummy lying on that stone."
Jack whispered in Katie's ear and
they both smiled. They went into
Harrods, and came out a few
minutes later with a small parcel.

Then they jumped on the bus and
travelled back to Trafalgar Square.

"This is for you," said Jack, handing him the parcel from Harrods. "We bought it with the last of our pocket money." The lion unwrapped it and laughed. "It's a woolly blanket!"

"It's to keep your tummy warm," said Katie.

"How kind you are," sighed the lion.

"Thanks for showing us London," said Jack.

"Next time I'll show you even more!" said the lion.

Then Katie saw Grandma was waking up.
The lion hopped onto his stone and kept
very still. And, as the sun went in,
he turned from gold to grey.
"Hello, you two," said Grandma.
"Shall we go off to see the sights now?"
"Oh!" said Katie. "I'm much too tired."
"I need a rest!" said Jack.
And they both flopped down
on a bench and fell asleep.

Get creative with Katie!

I loved my tour of London with the lion so much that
I drew some of my favourite sights from the day! Here they are.
Can you remember what they are all called?

If you go to London you could visit these
best spots too, and draw your own pictures.
I bet your drawings will be wonderful!
And remember, if you go to Trafalgar Square,
please wave to my friend, the lion.

Love Katie x